W9-CZK-589

Within the fairy tale treasure which has come into the world's possession, there is no doubt that Hans Christian Andersen's stories are of outstanding character. Their symbolism is rich with Christian values, and some of them are clear illustrations of the Gospel. From his early childhood in the town of Odense, Denmark, until his death in Copenhagen, Hans Christian Andersen (1805-1875) had a valid Christian faith which manifested itself in many of the approximately 150 stories and tales he wrote. In one of them, he said: "In every human life, whether poor or great, there is an invisible thread that shows we belong to God." The thread in Andersen's stories is one of optimism which has given hope and inspiration to people all over the world.

It is in this spirit that the Tales of Hans Christian Andersen are published. We are convinced of the validity of teaching spiritual principles and building character values through imaginative stories, just as Jesus used parables to teach the people of His time.

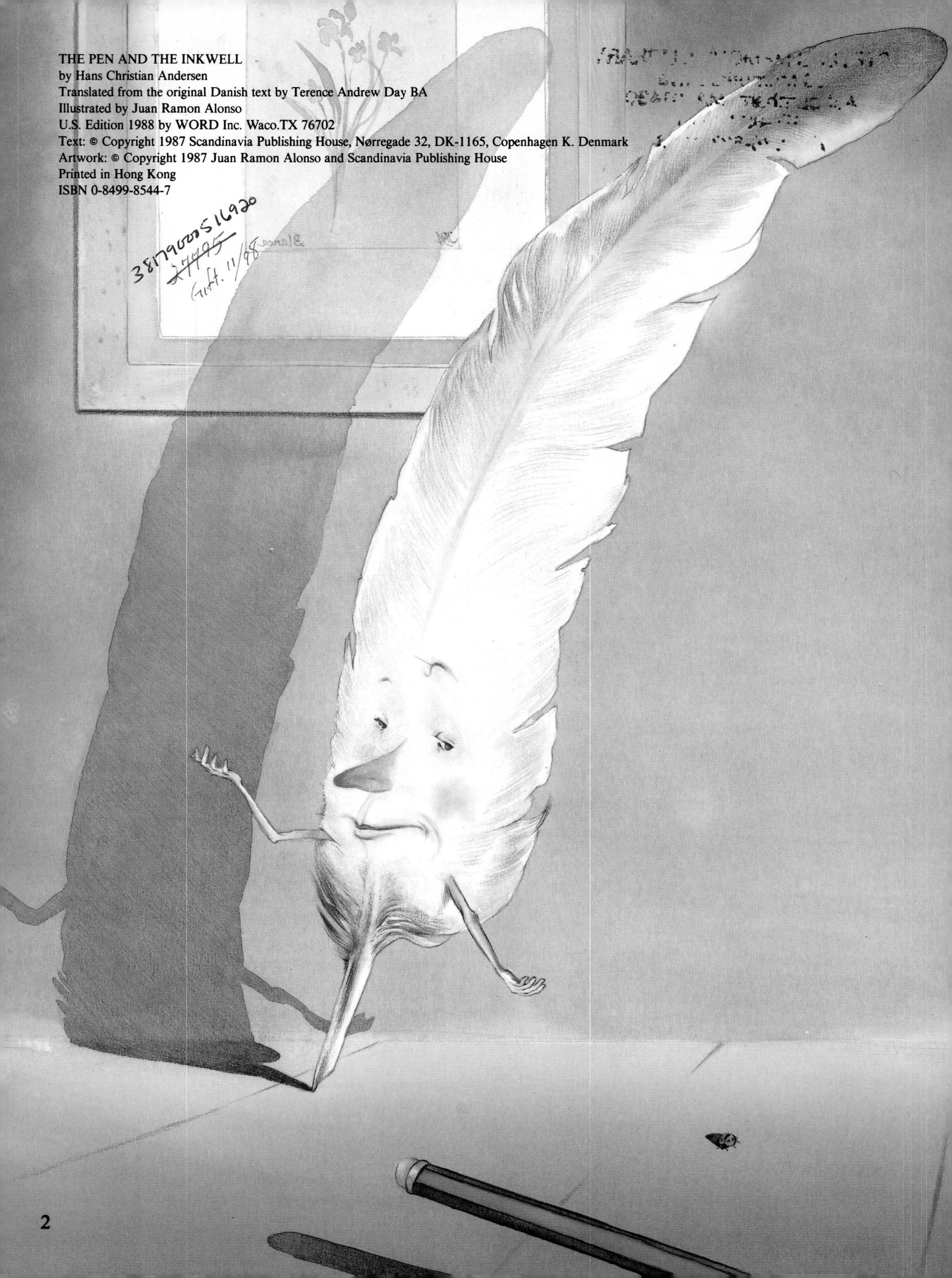

THE PEN AND THE INKWELL
by Hans Christian Andersen
Translated from the original Danish text by Terence Andrew Day BA
Illustrated by Juan Ramon Alonso
U.S. Edition 1988 by WORD Inc. Waco.TX 76702

Printed in Hong Kong
ISBN 0-8499-8544-7

The Pen and the Inkwell

Illustrated by Juan Ramon Alonso

Hans Christian Andersen

Translated for children from the original Danish text by Terence Andrew Day BA

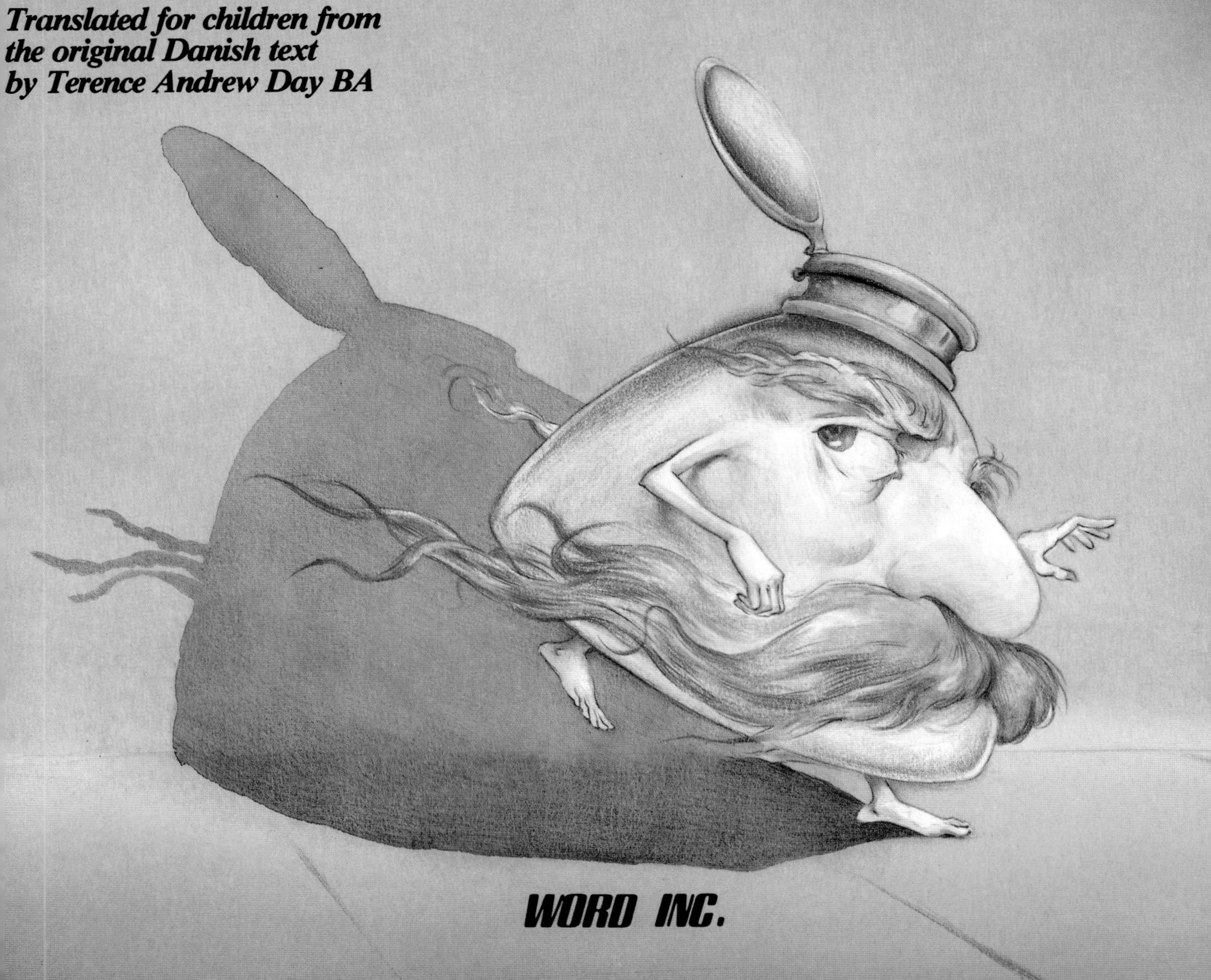

WORD INC.

It was evening in the room of a famous poet and everyone was watching the poet's inkwell, standing there on the desk.

Someone said, "Isn't it just wonderful, all the things that can come out of that inkwell! I wonder what he will come up with next? It is truly wonderful!"

"Yes, it certainly is," said the inkwell. "It is beyond all understanding as I always say!" He boasted to the quill pen and everyone else who could hear him on the desk.

"It is amazing, all the things that come out of me! Indeed it is almost unbelievable! and I honestly don't really know what will come next when the man begins drawing ink from me. One dip into me is enough to fill half a page of paper, just think of all the things which can be written on that!"

"I am really most extraordinary! All the great works of poets and writers, they all come from me! All those exciting characters people read about and think really exist."

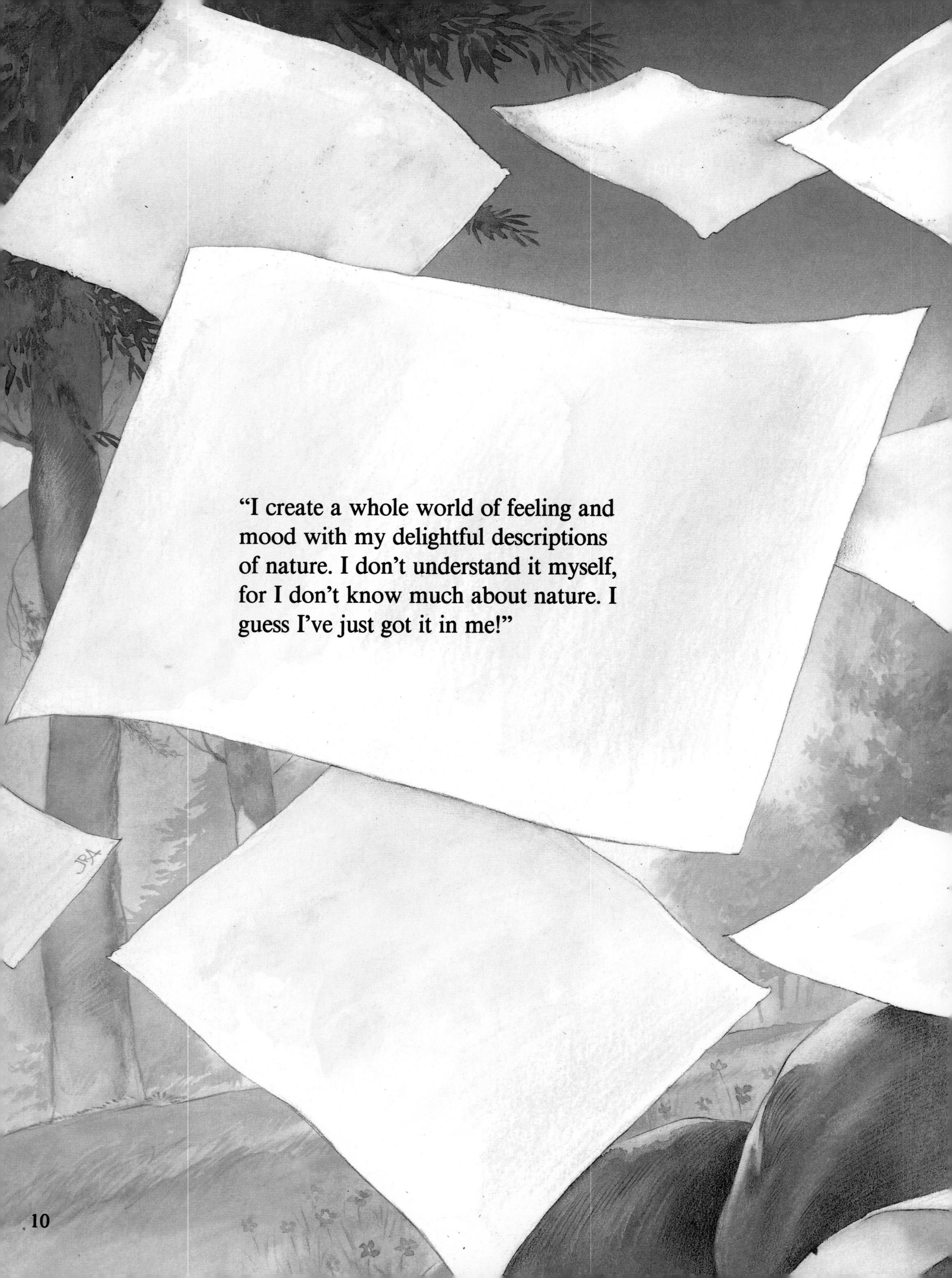

"I create a whole world of feeling and mood with my delightful descriptions of nature. I don't understand it myself, for I don't know much about nature. I guess I've just got it in me!"

"They all come out of me, all those tales of beautiful maidens and brave knights in shining armor coming to the rescue upon their great white stallions: King Arthur, Robin Hood, Sinbad the Sailor, whole armies of heroes and villains. I really can't remember them all. I assure you, I don't even have to think about it."

"You're right there!" the quill pen jeered, "You don't do any thinking at all. Because if you did, you would understand that you are just an ink-provider! You only supply the ink so I can think out and then make visible upon paper what I have in me, and that's what I write down. It is the pen that does the actual writing! There's no one that doubts that. And anyway, most people have just as much an understanding of poetry as an old inkwell."

20
PS

"What would you know about that! You have hardly any experience!" said the inkwell. "After all, you haven't worked here a week yet and you're already half worn-out. And you imagine that you're the real poet! You just do what you are told to do."

"I have seen the likes of you before you came, both from the goose family and British-made, too! I know all about both quills and steel pens! There have been many here in my employment and I'll have even more, when he, the man who writes with me, comes and puts down what he takes out of my insides. I would love to know what the first thing he takes out of me will be."

"Dumb inkpot!" said the pen.

Late in the evening the poet came home after having been to a concert. He had heard an excellent violinist and could think of nothing else but this musician's amazing performance. The violinist had produced a surprising richness of tones from the instrument. At times it had sounded like a shower of tinkling raindrops, one precious pearl falling upon another. Then it was like birds twittering merrily together.

JRA

Then finally the music rose in strength like the roar of a mighty wind rushing through a pine forest. The poet thought

he could hear his own heart weeping. It sounded just like a woman's soft voice singing.

To the audience it had seemed that the very violin strings had vibrated with music. Not only that, every single part of the instrument, including screws and joints had seemed to be part of the music. It was extraordinary! It was a difficult piece to perform, but the violinist made it look like child's play. The bow had merely glided back and forth over the strings. You would have thought that anyone at all could do the same, had they tried.

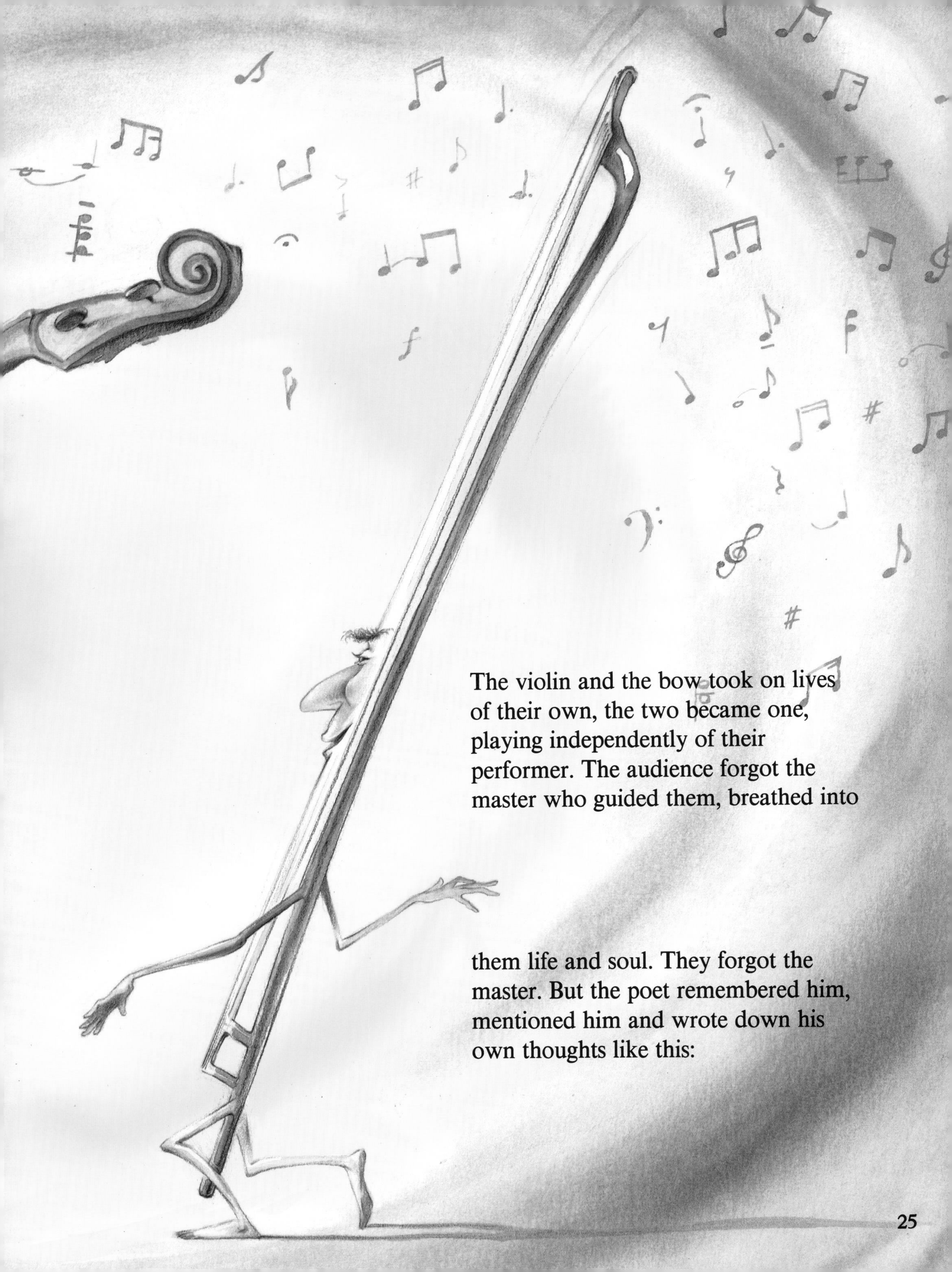

The violin and the bow took on lives of their own, the two became one, playing independently of their performer. The audience forgot the master who guided them, breathed into

them life and soul. They forgot the master. But the poet remembered him, mentioned him and wrote down his own thoughts like this:

"How foolish it would be, if the bow and the violin should brag about their performance! And yet this is just what we people do so often. The poet, the artist, the scientist, the general, we boast of our achievements. And yet we are nothing but instruments, on which our Lord is making music. To Him alone be the honor! We have nothing to boast of."

Indeed this was what the poet wrote down. He composed it as a parable and called it, 'The Master and the Instruments.'

"That'll teach you!" the pen sneered to the inkwell when they were both alone again. "Didn't you hear him read what I wrote?"

"Yes, you mean what I gave him to write," the inkwell corrected. "That will keep you from being so proud! Can't you see you are being made a fool of! That was a cut at you from within me! I should know when I'm being sarcastic."

"Stupid ink-container!" said the pen.

"Useless writing-stick!" said the inkwell.

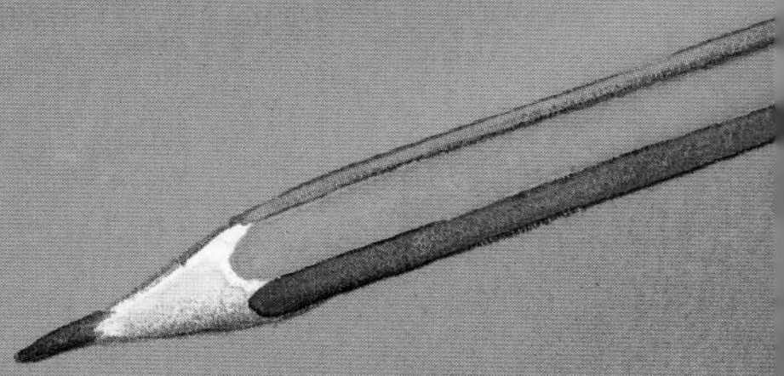

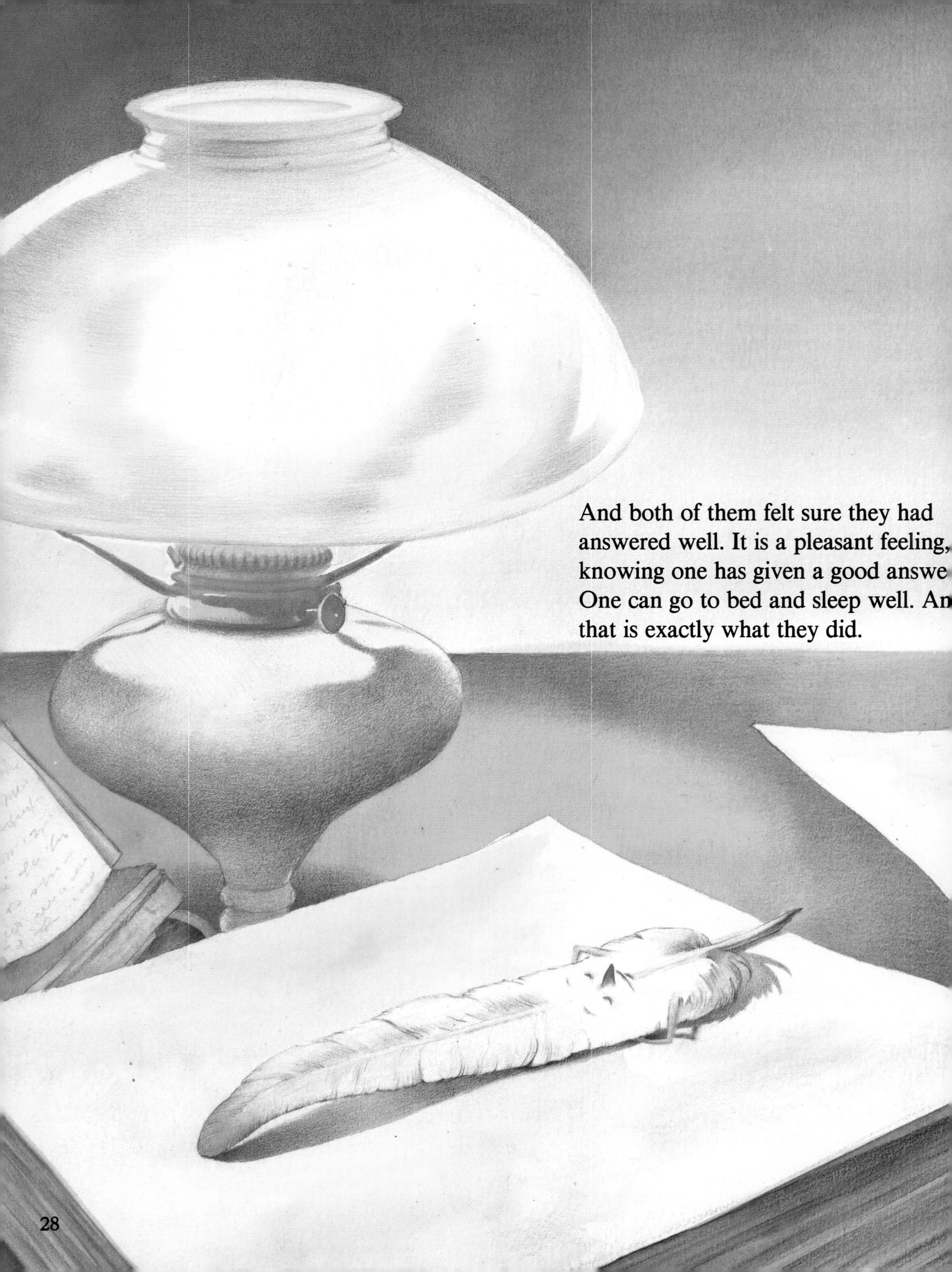

And both of them felt sure they had answered well. It is a pleasant feeling, knowing one has given a good answe One can go to bed and sleep well. An that is exactly what they did.

F&P

But the poet did not sleep. Thoughts kept emerging from his mind like the tones from the violin, dropping like pearls, rushing out like the storm through the forest. He could see his own heart in these thoughts. He could see a glimmer of light from the Eternal Master.

To Him alone be the honor!

Study Key

The Pen and the Inkwell

Explaining the story:

Here the pen, the inkwell, and the poet stand for something more than what they are in the story. The pen and inkwell could only think about how much more important one was than the other. Many people do this as well, and even argue about it just as the pen and the inkwell did. The wise poet tried to show them how they were really nothing more than instruments in the hands of their master, just as the violin could not play great music without the man who played the instrument. In turn, the poet knew he could only write great things with the help of God.

Talking about the truth of the story:

1. Did the pen and the inkwell learn the lesson the poet taught them? Why or why not?
2. Name some things you are in charge of. Who is in charge of you?
3. True greatness can often only happen once you accept yourself, without wanting selfishly to be the best at everything.
4. How were the violin's strings and bow different than the pen and the inkwell?

Applying the truth of the story:

1. Make a list of your talents, then list some things you wish you were better at. How is it possible to improve the skills on the first list? The second list?
2. How can you use your gifts to help other people?
3. Can you think of any "famous" people today who behave like the pen and the inkwell?